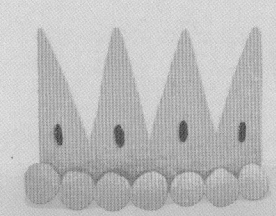

To Eddie, Benji and Pete, and my amazing mum
who wisely told me great things take time
— H R

To Nana, Grandad, Ma and Pop x
— S R

LITTLE TIGER PRESS LTD,
an imprint of the Little Tiger Group
1 Coda Studios, 189 Munster Road, London SW6 6AW
www.littletiger.co.uk

First published in Great Britain 2021

A CIP catalogue record for this book
is available from the British Library

Printed in China · LTP/2800/3506/1020

2 4 6 8 10 9 7 5 3 1

NEVER MESS
WITH A PIRATE
PRINCESS

Holly Ryan

Siân Roberts

LITTLE TIGER

LONDON

Princess Prudence loved her frog,
Her bunny and her spotty dog,
But nothing else could quite compare
To Little Ted, her royal bear.

She took him **here**,
she took him there,
She took that teddy
everywhere . . .

The supermarket

and the zoo . . .

She **even** took him to the **loo!**

But once upon a sunny day,
When all the knights went out to play,
The princess took a tiny nap
With Teddy sat upon her lap.

It truly was a BIG mistake,
For who should tiptoe past the lake,
With skull and crossbones on his chest,
A most unwanted palace guest!

He somersaulted through the air
And **snatched** the royal teddy bear.
Then, leaving Prudence fast asleep,

The pirate fled with one great LEAP!

"Teddy!" Princess Prudence sobbed.
"HELP!" she hollered, "I've been robbed!
Oh where, oh where could Teddy be?
I need him back immediately!"

Then, all at once, a gallant knight
Came charging up in armour bright.
"Fear not, Princess," he boldly said,
"I'm Brave Sir Frank – I'll save your Ted!"

"I don't suppose," asked Princess Prue,
"That I could ride along with you?
I'm more than just a little bored
And – look! – I even have a sword!"

"You? A knight? Oh, don't be daft!
You're FAR too small!" he rudely laughed.

But Princess Prue was not impressed.
She grabbed some things to help her quest.

Then in a flash, she jumped the moat,

And galloped off

on trusty GOAT!

She searched the woods where trees grow tall . . .

A magic glade . . .

a waterfall . . .

A rolling hill . . .

a sandy dune . . .

She searched
and searched *all*
afternoon.

And could she find that royal bear?
Sadly no, not **anywhere!**

But wait a minute, could it be

A pirate ship upon the sea?

And being poked along the plank

The NOT so bold, or brave, Sir Frank!

The pirates were a frightful sight
But Prudence was a fearless knight.
"I'll save you, Frank!" the princess cried,
Then off she swam against the tide . . .

Until with one almighty flip

She leapt on board the pirate ship!

"WHO GOES THERE?"

the pirates roared,

But Prue was quick

and drew her sword.

She tied the pirates to the mast
As Brave Sir Frank just watched aghast.
And there, inside a treasure chest,

She found her bear with royal crest!

Now Princess Prue was firm but fair.
"You pirates can't pinch teddy bears –
They're very precious friends," she said.
"Stick to things that shine instead!"

"We're sorry!"
cried the naughty brutes.
"They're just so soft and awful cute!
But 'cos you're cross, we'll pack a sack
And take them teddies safely back."

And since good pirates NEVER fib,

That's just exactly what they did.

And now I hear that Princess Prue's

A knight in shining armour too,

But often likes to take a trip

As captain of the pirate ship.

And while the crew look after Frog,

Her bunny and her spotty dog,

She hunts for treasure far and wide

With Teddy safely by her side.